Library of Congress Cataloging-in-Publication Data: Schade, Susan.   Snug house, bug house / by Susan Schade and Jon Buller.   p.   cm.   — (A Bright and early book)   SUMMARY: Six bugs find a tennis ball and turn it into a wonderful house for themselves.   ISBN 0-679-85300-6 (trade) — ISBN 0-679-95300-0 (lib. bdg.)   [1. Insects—Fiction.   2. Dwellings—Fiction.   3. Stories in rhyme.]   I. Buller, Jon.   II. Title.   III. Series: Bright & early book.   PZ8.3.S287Sn   1994   [E]—dc20   93-34058

Manufactured in the United States of America   10 9 8 7 6 5 4 3

GROLIER
BOOK CLUB EDITION

SNUG HOUSE, BUG HOUSE!

by Susan Schade and Jon Buller

A Bright & Early Book
From BEGINNER BOOKS
A Division of Random House, Inc.

Find it

Think it

Plan it

Ink it

Scoop it

Smash it

Push it

Mash it

Mix it

Pour it

Smooth it

Floor it

Roll it

Stop it

Saw it

Drop it

Cut it

Glue it

Stir it

Fill it

Paint it

Spill it

Roof it

Wire it

Finish it
Admire it!

Ed's room

Fred's room

Ann's room

Fran's room

Spot's room

Dot's room

Crazy room

Lazy room

Sound room

Round room

Small house
Ball house
Snug house
Bug house!